WHAT MAKES A COMMUNITY?

HOSPITALS

by J. P. Press

Consultant: Marla Conn, Reading Specialist, Read-Ability

BEARPORT PUBLISHING

Minneapolis, Minnesota

Teaching Tips

Before Reading

- Look at the cover of the book. Discuss the picture and the title.
- Ask readers to brainstorm a list of what they already know about the hospital. What can they expect to see in this book?
- Go on a picture walk, looking through the pictures to discuss vocabulary and make predictions about the text.

During Reading

- Read for purpose. Encourage readers to think about the hospital and its role in the community as they are reading.
- Ask readers to think about the setting of the book. Where does the story take place?
- Ask readers to look for the details of the story. What is happening?
- If readers encounter an unknown word, ask them to look at the sounds in the word. Then, ask them to look at the rest of the page. Are there any clues to help them understand?

After Reading

- Encourage readers to pick a buddy and reread the book together.
- Ask readers to name three things from this book that they could find at a hospital. Go back and find the pages that tell about these things.
- Ask readers to write and draw a picture about something they learned about the hospital.

Credits:
Cover and title page, © Spiroview Inc/Shutterstock; 3, © Digital Storm/Shutterstock; 5, © buzbuzzer/iStock; 7, © Hispanolistic/iStock; 8, © Sue Wetjen/Dreamstime; 11, © RGB Ventures/SuperStock/Alamy Stock Photo; 13, © fizkes/Shutterstock; 14, © Alina555/Getty Images; 17, © FatCamera/iStock; 18, © upixa/Shutterstock; 21, © monkeybusinessimages/iStock; 22, © Rocketclips, Inc./Shutterstock; 23BL, © Gorodenkoff/Shutterstock; 23BM, © Aquarius Studio/Shutterstock; 23BR, © itsmejust/Shutterstock; 23TL, © Monkey Business Images/Shutterstock; 23TM, © Peakstock/Shutterstock; 23TR, © Rost-9D/iStock

Library of Congress Cataloging-in-Publication Data

Names: Press, J. P., 1993– author.
Title: Hospitals / J.P. Press ; consultant Marla Conn.
Description: Bearcub books. | Minneapolis, Minnesota : Bearport Publishing Company, [2021] | Series: What makes a community? | Includes bibliographical references and index.
Identifiers: LCCN 2020029812 (print) | LCCN 2020029813 (ebook) | ISBN 9781647474461 (library binding) | ISBN 9781647474546 (paperback) | ISBN 9781647474621 (ebook)
Subjects: LCSH: Hospitals—Juvenile literature. | Medical personnel—Juvenile literature. | Medical care—Juvenile literature.
Classification: LCC RA963.5 .P74 2021 (print) | LCC RA963.5 (ebook) | DDC 362.11—dc23
LC record available at https://lccn.loc.gov/2020029812
LC ebook record available at https://lccn.loc.gov/2020029813

For more information, write to Bearport Publishing, 5357 Penn Avenue South, Minneapolis, MN 55419.

Printed in the United States of America.

Contents

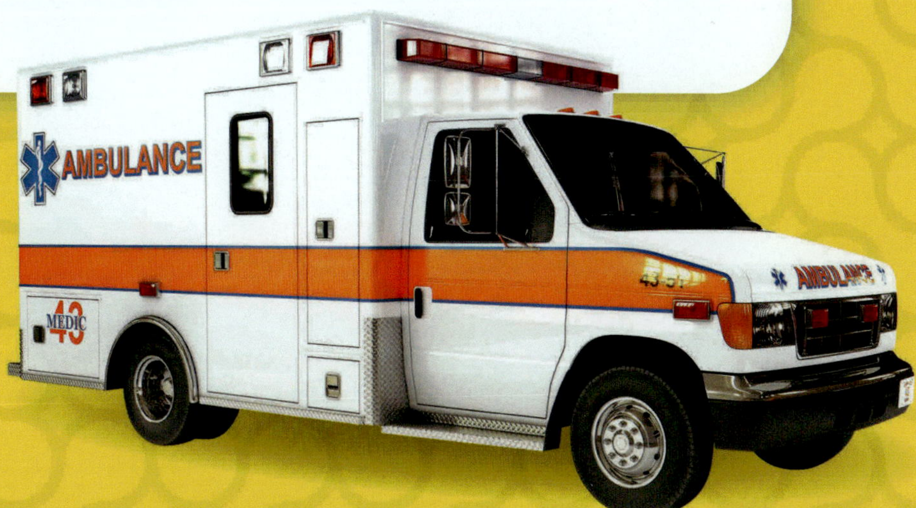

The New Hospital

There is a new hospital in our **community**.

Sick people will go there.

Doctors will help make them better.

It is time to look inside!

5

First, you need to check in.

That way the hospital knows you are there.

Go to the front desk.

The TOOTH Book

Next, you wait.

There is a lot to do in the waiting room.

You can play with games and read books.

Then, it is time to go to an **exam** room.

You talk to a doctor.

They ask what is wrong.

Tell them how you feel.

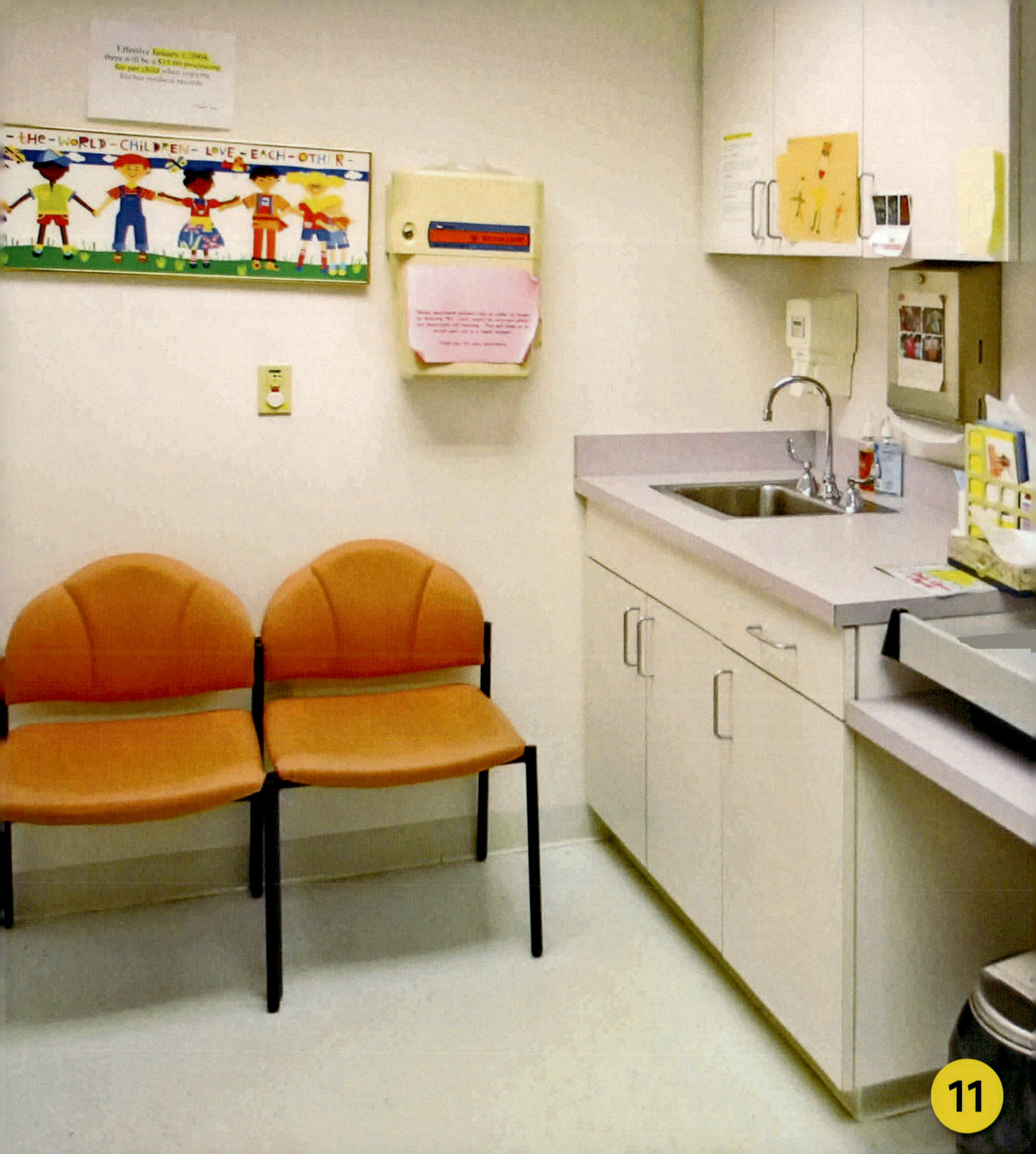
THE-WORLD-CHILDREN-LOVE-EACH-OTH R

Sometimes, the doctor wants to do **tests**.

The tests tell the doctor more about you.

An x-ray

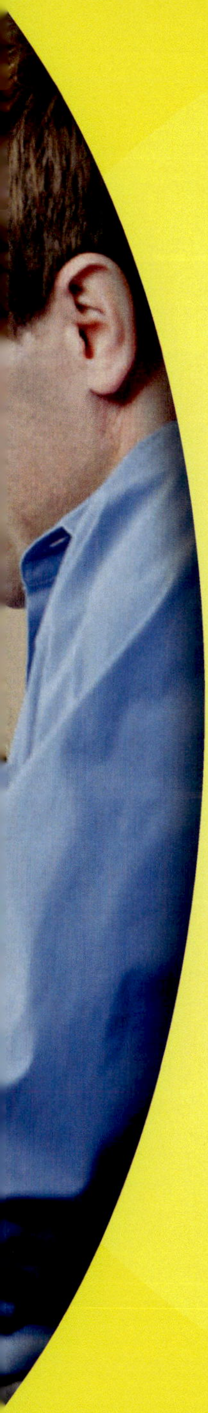

The doctor may take an **x-ray**.

An x-ray sees inside your body.

It can show if you have broken bones.

Some tests can show if you are sick.

These tests are done at the hospital **lab**.

The workers use tools.

They see if you have **germs**.

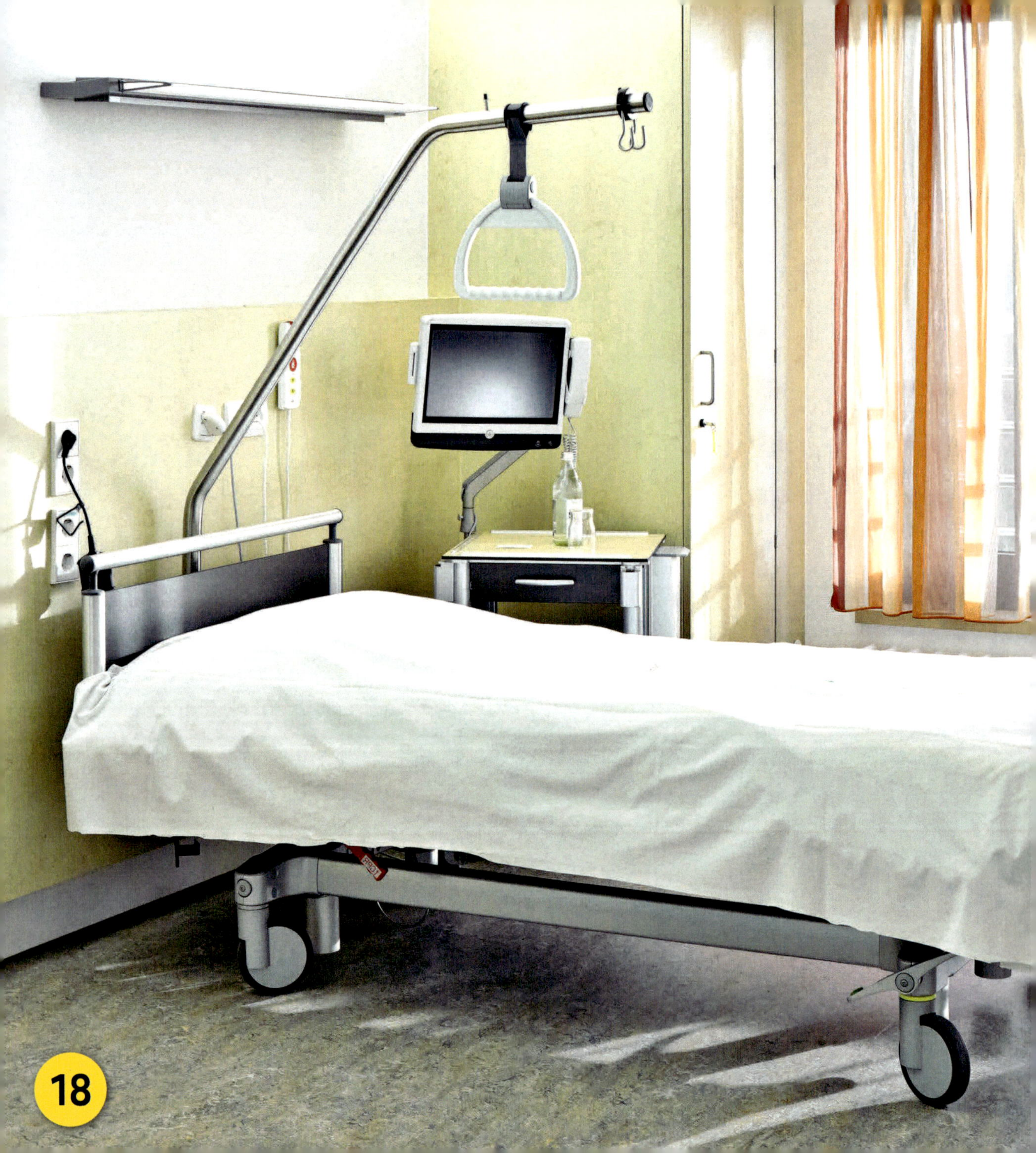

18

Sick people may stay at the hospital.

There are rooms for them.

Each room has a bed.

Sometimes there is a TV, too.

That was a great trip.

The new hospital is very nice.

It will help a lot of people get better!

At the Hospital

Glossary

community the people and places in an area where people live

exam when a doctor looks closely at a person

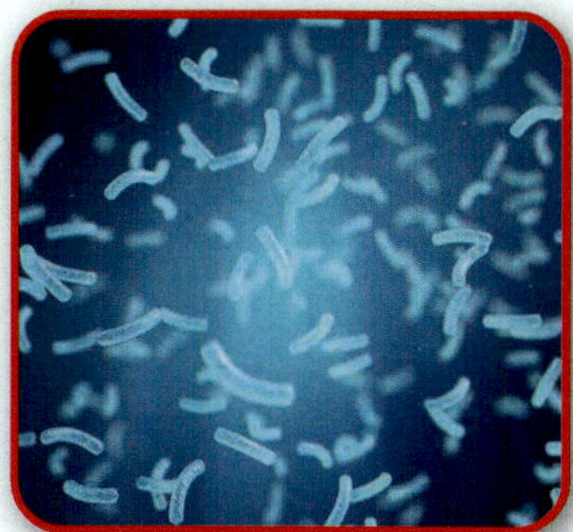

germs tiny living things that can make you sick

lab a place with special tools where tests are done

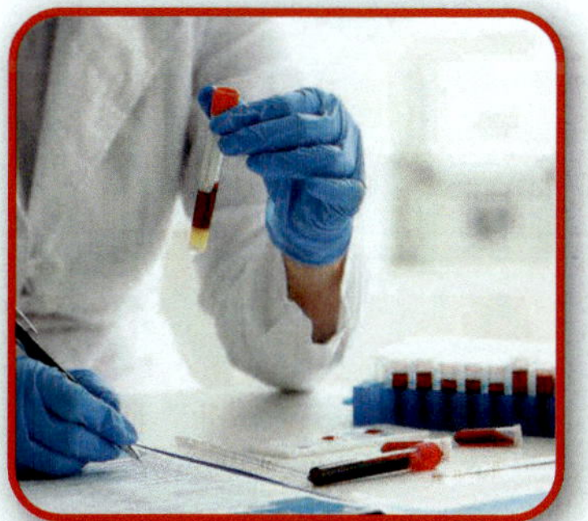

tests close looks at a part of the body or something taken from the body

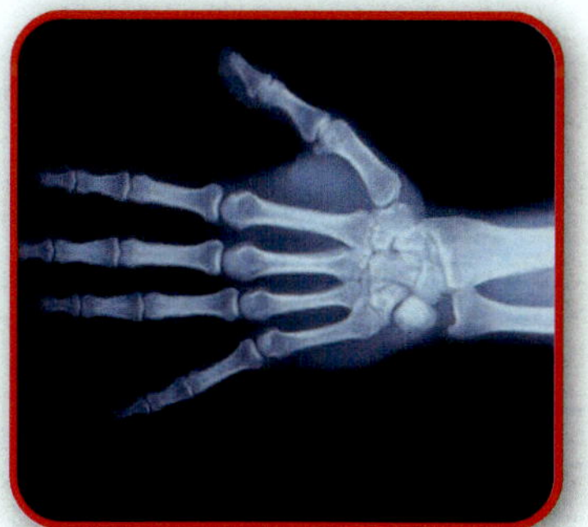

x-ray a picture of the inside of a body

Index

Read More

Brinker, Spencer. *Doctors (What Makes a Community?).* Minneapolis: Bearport, 2021.

Clark, Rosalyn. *Why We Go to the Hospital (Bumba Books—Health Matters).* Minneapolis: Lerner Publications, 2018.

Learn More Online

1. Go to **www.factsurfer.com**
2. Enter "**Hospitals Community**" into the search box.
3. Click on the cover of this book to see a list of websites.

About the Author

J. P. Press likes to run, read, and help her community in any way she can!